THAT'S A JOB?

I like ANIMALS

... what jobs are there?

by Steve Martin

Illustrated by Roberto Blefari

Kane Miller
A DIVISION OF EDC PUBLISHING

CONTENTS

Pet photographer 25

Animal actor agent 26

Wildlife filmmaker 27

Wildlife conservationist 28

Marine biologist 30

Zoo vet 32

Mounted police officer 34

Zookeeper (primates) 36

Zookeeper (reptiles) 38

Zoologist 40

Entomologist 41

Animal control officer 42

Kennel attendant 43

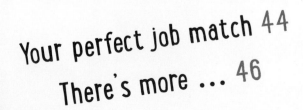

INTRODUCTION

Qualities and skills for working with animals

There are lots of jobs working with animals, some of which you may not even know existed.

From jobs in science, conservation and charity, to the police and the arts—there are many opportunities for people who want to work with animals.

Each job needs different people with different skills: zoologists and marine biologists have to go to college for a long time to gain qualifications; kennel attendants must show that they are used to being around dogs, while pet photographers need artistic skills.

But there are some qualities that everyone who works with animals should have: a kind, caring personality and, most importantly, a love of animals and a real passion to help them. This is why a vet jumps out of bed on a cold night to go help a sick horse, and why a zookeeper gives as much care and attention to a tiny frog as they would to a huge giraffe.

A love of learning is important too. The more you know about animals, the better you can care for them. Sometimes you might need to be quite brave as well—you may have to stand up to others or face danger to save and protect animals. And you'll always need to be ready to do the yuckier tasks too. Imagine how much poop an elephant keeper needs to clean up every day!

Whatever the job, the animals must always come first. Whether you want to work in a zoo, a pet store, a rescue center or a stable, it's important to remember that the animals will depend on you for their health and happiness, so you must want the very best for them.

If all this sounds like you, then you're the right type of person to work with animals!

This book looks at 25 different jobs that involve working with animals, giving you a sneak peek into a typical day in the life of each worker. You'll learn the important stuff, like what it takes to get the job and what duties and tasks are involved, and you'll discover the fun stuff too, such as the best part of a pet vet's day and what really bugs an entomologist ...

HINT: It involves insects flying up their nose!

When you've read about all the different jobs in the book, turn to page 44 to find out which jobs might suit you, or page 46 to discover even more jobs!

PET VET

Pets are precious to their owners, and my job is to make sure these much-loved animals are happy and healthy. I treat cats, dogs, snakes, turtles, rabbits, birds and many more! The one thing that always stays the same is my compassion; to be a good vet you have to care about your patients.

I'm trained to treat a variety of pets, but they tend to be no bigger than your average dog. Zoo vets (see pages 32–33) and large animal vets (see pages 16–17) look after much bigger animals.

3

My next job is to operate on a cat called Sammy. I'll need the nurse to help me. We examine our patient and give him some anesthetic, which puts him to sleep and stops him from feeling any pain. While I operate, the nurse monitors Sammy closely, checking his heart rate and breathing.

2

The first job doesn't take long. I just need to give a puppy its vaccinations; these injections will protect her from diseases.

VETERINARY

1

My day starts with looking through the appointments with our receptionist. It looks like I'm in for a busy day!

4

After the operation, we keep an eye on our patient to make sure there are no further problems. When his owner arrives, I'll tell her how to care for Sammy for the next few days and explain why he needs to keep the plastic collar on—so that he doesn't pull out the surgery stitches.

5

Most appointments are scheduled, but there are always emergencies. I have to act quickly when a man rushes in with his parrot, which has been attacked by a cat. Luckily, Polly isn't badly hurt, but I need to dress the wound and give her some medicine to make sure there is no infection.

6

Fortunately, there are no more surprises, and I spend a few hours giving medicines and carrying out health checks. I also give advice to owners about their pet's food and behavior. I have to know so much about so many animals in my job. This is why training to be a vet lasts for around eight years and involves a lot of hard study.

7

My next appointment is with Hamish, a wriggly little hamster. His owner has brought him in to have his teeth filed. Hamsters' teeth never stop growing, so it's important to file them so they don't injure themselves.

8

The last visit of the day is from a man who thinks his dog, Lulu, might be having puppies. I carry out an ultrasound scan which shows three tiny babies inside. We'll need to keep an eye on things, so we schedule another appointment before they leave.

MY JOB: BEST AND WORST PARTS

BEST: I help pets to get well and stay well.

WORST: It's not possible to save every sick animal, and it's heartbreaking when owners have to say a last goodbye to their pets.

POLICE DOG HANDLER

Most police officers work with a partner. Mine is called Spike, and he has four legs and a tail! Together we protect our community. I worked hard to get my job, and I had to do specialist training and work as a regular police officer before I could join the canine unit.

Dogs don't just help the police. You'll find dogs and their handlers working with the army, in security services and with mountain rescue teams. They sniff out explosives, guard buildings and track down lost or injured civilians.

3

Once we're there, I let Spike out and we head into the woods. I know that if the suspect is still here, Spike will find them. I was Spike's trainer when he was a puppy, and we spent hours together practicing his tracking skills.

1

My first job of the day is to give Spike breakfast. He's a large German shepherd with a healthy appetite and needs lots of protein in his diet. Afterward, I take him to a park where we play fetch before we set off for work. Chasing after the ball is great exercise.

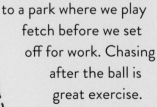

2

At the station, we pick up our patrol car which is designed especially for dogs, with a large cage in the back. We don't have to wait long for the first call for help. A thief has escaped into the woods and needs to be found.

4

German shepherds have a superstrong sense of smell, and they can be trained to track objects and people. Spike lifts his nose to the air and sniffs the ground too. He soon leads us to the culprit, who is led off to the station.

5

I make sure to praise Spike for his good work, and it isn't long before the next call comes in. Another police team has cornered a burglar in a backyard, but the man is waving a large stick at them and refusing to surrender.

6

When we arrive, I warn the suspect that, unless he drops the stick and comes quietly, I'll let the dog off his leash. Spike is trained to grab suspects by biting them on the arm and holding on until I give the command to let go. The burglar takes one look at Spike and, very sensibly, drops his weapon.

7

After lunch, we visit a school where I talk to the children about my job. Spike is very well behaved and enjoys all the attention.

8

Finally, it's the end of the day. I change out of my uniform, call for Spike, and we head home. You really have to love dogs in my job because Spike isn't just my colleague—we live together too!

MY JOB: BEST AND WORST PARTS

BEST: My job is really exciting. I never know what challenges are waiting for me.

WORST: I have to keep fit so that I can keep up with my partner. He's got twice as many legs to run with!

DOG GROOMER

I became a dog groomer after struggling to cut my own dog's hair. That led me to take a dog-grooming course. I loved it so much that I decided to make a career out of it. It's a very rewarding job, but it can be a messy business too!

I work in a pet-grooming salon which employs a number of groomers. Not all groomers work in salons; some work in pet stores or kennels, or travel to pet owners' homes.

1

My first client is a regular. He's a cute cairn terrier called Woody. He always leaves my salon looking perfect, but comes back a few months later with long, straggly, knotted hair.

2

Today, Woody's here for the works: ear cleaning, bath and shampoo, coat trim and nail clipping. Some dogs get nervous, so I need to be calm and soothing to help them relax. There's no trouble with Woody, though—he loves being pampered.

3

My next client is a komondor called Lola. Komondors have very unusual coats and can look a little like mops! In my job, you have to know how to groom all breeds of dogs, so I know how to get Lola looking her best. Her "cords" can't be brushed, but they still need to be kept clean and parasite free.

MY JOB: BEST AND WORST PARTS

BEST: I love keeping dogs beautiful and healthy.

WORST: All the hair! You wouldn't believe how much sweeping I have to do.

4

The last dog of the day is Frida, a bichon frise puppy. She's a little nervous, so another groomer helps keep her calm while I trim her coat. It takes longer than cutting a human's hair and needs lots of patience. At last, Frida's ready for home, and after some cleaning up, I am too.

GUIDE DOG TRAINER

When a relative of mine lost their eyesight, I learned about guide dogs. I like helping others, and I adore dogs, so I was very interested. I volunteered at shelters, took classes in college and started working with a charity. Now I'm a qualified trainer and I have no regrets.

I get to work with different dog breeds in my job. Golden retrievers, Labrador retrievers and German shepherds are the most common. They're easy to train and they just love human company.

1

This morning I'm making my way along a busy street, blindfolded! I'm with Pixie, a guide dog I've been working with for months, and this is part of her training. I can hear the roar of cars whooshing past, but I'm not frightened. I know Pixie will help me stay safe.

2

I'm thrilled when she confidently avoids obstacles, stops at the side of the road and gets on and off the bus. It's been hard work to train her to such a high standard, but it means she will be a trusted companion to her new owner.

MY JOB: BEST AND WORST PARTS

BEST: I love seeing owners and dogs working as a team. Guide dogs change people's lives, and I'm thankful to be a part of that.

WORST: I build strong bonds with the dogs, so it can be hard to say goodbye.

3

I spend the rest of the day introducing a client to her future guide dog, Bailey. They'll have to train together for four weeks before they're ready to live and work as a team. The meeting goes well, and we try a few exercises. I can tell it's going to be a great match!

OUR BEST FRIENDS

Not all assistance dogs are guide dogs. There are autism service dogs, seizure response dogs and many more. Assistance dogs can be super helpful; they can open doors and bring their owners belongings like keys and wallets.

STABLE MANAGER

I have lots of duties and very long days in my job! I worked my way up to my role over a number of years, starting as a groom taking care of the stables. I then worked closely with the previous stable manager to learn all I could about horses, running a business and managing a team. Then I finally got the job.

I never get bored in my job. I'm a jockey, an animal nurse, a repairman, a businessman ... whatever needs doing!

1

My day begins at 5:00 a.m. The sun isn't even up yet, but that's when the horses want to be fed, so that's when the team starts.

4

I head back to the office to call the farrier (a specialist in horses' hooves) and arrange for him to come fit new shoes to two of the horses.

2

I have a new groom starting today (a groom is someone who looks after horses). I start by showing her how to feed the horses. Next, I show her how to muck out the stables, which involves clearing out the horse poop. After she's done this, there will be all the riding equipment to clean, as well as putting the saddles on the horses.

3

My next task is to visit our horse whisperer. He's working with our new stallion, Blue. Horse whisperers spend years studying horses. They learn to understand the meaning of every tail swish and hoof stomp. Most of all, they know how to win a horse's trust. Blue was very anxious and frightened when he first arrived, but after just a few weeks, he's already much calmer.

5

The duties don't stop. Once I'm off the phone, I welcome the horse dentist, who has arrived to check our large, black mare Milly's teeth. It's my job to make sure all our horses are healthy, so I often arrange for specialists to come.

6

By now it's 11:00 a.m. and the day's first students are arriving for their riding lessons. The instructor collects the horses and leads them into the paddock. Whichever horses aren't ridden by the students will still need exercise, so the grooms and I will take them out later. I don't mind—riding the horses is my favorite part of the day!

7

I leave the instructor with her class and spend the afternoon in the office, ordering food supplies, scheduling vet visits and paying bills. At 3:00 p.m. we take the unexercised horses for a ride. The grooms race each other over the fields, and we head back as the sun sets.

8

I get ready to leave the office at 5:30 p.m. Before I go, I visit the stables to check that the grooms have brushed down the horses and all is well. I don't have far to go; I actually live here! I can stay late if I need to, or be on hand in case of emergencies.

MY JOB: BEST AND WORST PARTS

BEST: I love helping out at our riding school—seeing people learn to ride and develop their understanding of horses is awesome.

WORST: Sometimes I spend too much time in the office, when I'd rather be out riding.

WILDLIFE SANCTUARY MANAGER

I don't have to travel far to my job at Rocky Mountain Wildlife Sanctuary because I live here! We treat sick animals, then release them back into the wild when they're better. I started out as a volunteer, and now my job is to make sure everyone who works here does what they need to do to help the animals recover quickly.

It's easy for people to forget that wild animals can get sick or injured in the same way as pets can, and that someone has to care for these animals. In a typical year, we help over 2,000 animals: everything from cougars to mountain goats!

1

Every day starts with a team meeting with the rehabilitation specialist, the wildlife education officer, our two fundraisers and the vet. We go through our tasks for the day. Being able to work well together is really important because there is always so much to do.

2

After the meeting, I check in with the rehabilitation specialist. She treats injured animals. She tells me about a bald eagle she thinks has been poisoned from eating lead bullets used by hunters. I ask her to keep me updated, and I leave her to run some tests.

3

I tour the sanctuary and visit our four orphaned grizzly bear cubs. I listen to our wildlife education officer giving a talk to a group of visiting schoolchildren. We stay well away from the cubs—we don't want them getting used to people, as they will be returning to the wild when they are ready to fend for themselves.

4

Next, I check the aviary—a large enclosure where the birds are kept. I make sure the birds are all fed and watered, including our new patient—a ptarmigan with a broken wing. Not all our birds live here, though. We have two injured Canada geese at our small lake. They will simply fly away when they're ready.

5

I head to the office where one of our fundraisers is sending an update on an injured moose to a local school that has been raising money for us. Our fundraisers work hard to persuade the public to donate money so that the sanctuary can stay open. They don't work directly with the animals, but their job is just as important.

6

I decide to visit the vet next, to check how the moose is recovering. She was brought in with a broken leg after running onto a busy road and being hit by a car. It's good news—the vet has fixed the moose's leg, and we'll be able to return her to the woodland as soon as she is able to stand.

MY JOB: BEST AND WORST PARTS

BEST: It's wonderful to be able to release animals back into the wild where they belong.

WORST: We're often under pressure to raise enough money to help the animals.

7

I finish the day with a meeting with two new volunteers. One wants to work as a guide for visitors, and the other wants to work with the animals. We always need plenty of help at the sanctuary!

LARGE ANIMAL VET

I've always loved animals. In fact, I used to spend my weekends helping out at the local shelter. I also love being outdoors, so this job was the obvious choice for me. After veterinary school, I joined a vet practice, and today I split my days between the office and visiting farms and ranches, helping farmers keep their animals healthy.

1

It's 8:30 a.m. and I'm driving my truck along a country road with Buster, my collie. I'm headed to a farm where one of the farmer's sheep is struggling to give birth. With a helping hand, I make sure the lamb arrives safely and the mother is well, before setting off for our next call.

I'm trained to look after large animals, such as cows, pigs, sheep and horses. Some large animal vets specialize in just one animal, such as cows (known as a bovine veterinarian) or horses (equine veterinarian). Pet vets (see pages 6–7) look after smaller animals.

2

Blue Valley is a large dairy farm run by the Emmerson family. Together, we spend an hour vaccinating their cows. Vaccinations are injections that stop the spread of disease and are really important when a lot of animals are living together.

3

After letting Buster have a run around, we jump back into the truck and head off to the next call. I need a large vehicle like this because I have to carry all my equipment with me—it's like a vet's office on wheels!

4

We arrive at Oakland Ranch where Jess, a beautiful gray horse, is limping painfully. I examine her leg carefully— I don't want to get a nasty kick! I find a small infected wound, so I clean it out, bandage her leg and give her some medicine to stop the infection.

5

We spend the afternoon visiting more farms. I treat pigs infected with a skin disease, check a herd of cows to see which are pregnant, and carry out blood tests on a pair of goats.

6

My last visit of the day is to the veterinary office, where I can make phone calls to clients, check emails and write up reports about the animals I've treated.

7

Finally, after giving Buster a walk, we head off home as the sun sets behind the hills. It's the end of another long day …

MY JOB: BEST AND WORST PARTS

BEST: I love spending most of my time out in the fresh (sometimes stinky!) air.

WORST: I have to be ready for any emergency at any time—even at night, or during a storm.

8

The phone rings at 4:00 a.m. A farmer has spotted a sick pig. I crawl out of bed and get dressed. Ten minutes later, I'm driving to the farm in the pouring rain. I hope I'm offered a cup of coffee!

PET ADOPTION COUNSELOR

Animal rescue centers look after abandoned, stray or sick animals, and try to find new homes for them. I began working at New Start Animal Rescue Center five years ago as a volunteer. After college, I took a job as a pet adoption counselor, to help match people to their perfect pet.

> The rescue center where I work cares for dogs and cats, but other rescue centers look after rabbits and hamsters, or larger animals like horses and donkeys. These animals might have been treated badly or grown too old for their owners to look after them.

2

I watch and wait as the vet vaccinates Walker (to protect him from diseases) and checks that he doesn't have fleas or worms—it's important that parasites don't spread among our animals.

1

The first person I see when I arrive at work is the vet. She's checking over our new arrival: a little dog we've named Walker. He's a mutt (meaning he's a mix of different dog breeds) and he was brought in yesterday by an animal control officer after someone phoned to report an abandoned dog wandering around town.

3

Afterward, I spend some time getting to know Walker. I need to know our animals' personalities very well so I can find the most suitable owners for them. Finally, I take him to a kennel where he can eat, drink and rest safely.

4

Next, I have a talk with a man looking for a pet cat. I ask if he has other pets, and what his lifestyle is like. In the end, we decide on Pearl, a shy old cat—the man has plenty of time to give her lots of attention so I'm confident it's the right choice.

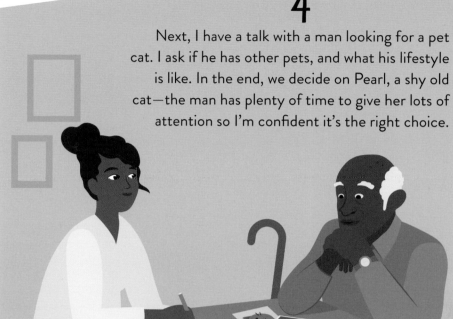

5

After lunch, I speak to a couple who would like a cat. They already have three spaniels at home, so I need to think carefully about the best match for them. I wouldn't want to send a nervous kitten home with three lively dogs! I schedule another meeting and start a list of possible matches.

6

The next part of my day is spent answering emails and writing reports about the animals. I make a phone call to an owner who has recently taken home one of our rescue dogs, to check how things are working out.

7

The last job of the day is saying goodbye to Ruby, a friendly tabby cat who is leaving with her new owners. I've matched her with a family with two young children who will love playing with her. I give them some advice about looking after her and wave them off. It's a happy ending to another busy day!

MY JOB: BEST AND WORST PARTS

BEST: Helping animals find a new home is the best feeling in the world.

WORST: Sadly, not every animal can be rehomed.

DOG WALKER

As a dog lover who enjoys walking, this is the perfect job for me! I started out by walking dogs for friends. The word soon spread, and now I walk up to 15 dogs a day! I have to learn about different breeds and how they behave, so I can keep the dogs safe and happy when we're out and about.

Dog walkers can also offer extra services to their clients, like pet sitting (see opposite page), or having dogs to stay overnight.

1

My job is to pick up the dogs from their homes and walk them while their owners are at work. Before I leave the house, I check that I've got everything: the dog owners' house keys, spare leashes, water and lots of poop bags! I always check the weather forecast too.

2

I drive around to collect the first dogs. I usually walk three dogs together. I know which ones get on well and which ones don't. All dogs love a walk, so there's a lot of excited tail wagging to welcome me.

3

Once I've collected the dogs, I drive to the big park downtown. It takes about 45 minutes to walk around the park. Then I take the dogs home and drive on to pick up the next group of excited customers.

4

On a typical day, I complete four or five walks. By the time I'm finished, I'm ready to go home and put my feet up!

MY JOB: BEST AND WORST PARTS

BEST: Having so many doggie friends is a dream come true!

WORST: It's not so much fun being outside in the pouring rain.

PET SITTER

I started pet sitting because I want to be a vet, and it's a great way to get some hands-on experience. With my mom's permission, I pet sit for neighbors when they go on vacation. It's really important to do a good job so that people trust you and ask you back again.

I mostly look after dogs and cats, but I also pet sit rabbits, parrots and even fish. I feed them, check that they have fresh water and spend time playing and chatting with them.

1

Today I get up early so that I can stop by a neighbor's house on my way to school. I'm here to feed his cats, Poppy and Patches, while he's away. We play with their favorite toy, then I head off to school.

2

After school, I walk over to another neighbor's house to feed their pet parrot. He's very noisy and likes to chat! I fill up his bowl with seeds and carefully place it inside his cage so I don't frighten him.

3

The last stop of the day is my next-door neighbors' house to feed their rabbit, Archie. He's quite shy and always hides when I arrive. But he soon appears when he realizes it's dinnertime.

4

After I arrive home, there's a knock at the door. It's my mom's friend with Lizzie, a little Jack Russell terrier. The friend is going away for the night and has asked me to look after Lizzie, who gets upset if she has to go to a kennel. I love having Lizzie for a sleepover!

MY JOB: BEST AND WORST PARTS

BEST: I can do this job while I'm still in school!

WORST: Some pets need to be fed more than once a day, so I have to be really organized with my time.

4

Next, I head off to check Billy, a young chimpanzee who has just arrived from another zoo. He will be kept apart from the other animals while we check that he isn't carrying any illnesses that could be passed on. Luckily, he has no signs of health problems.

5

In the afternoon, I hear some exciting news: our golden frogs' eggs have started hatching! Golden frogs are extinct (there are none left) in the wild, so we have begun a program to breed more frogs. I advise the keeper on what to feed the new little tadpoles and how to keep them healthy.

MY JOB: BEST AND WORST PARTS

BEST: There's a lot of variety in my work—every day is different.

WORST: Zoo vets have to study and train for several years because of the wide range of animals they will be working with. But it's worth all that hard work.

6

After helping a giraffe with a limp and a sick penguin, it's time to finish for the day. When I get home and my children ask me what I did at work, I tell them that my patients included tadpoles, elephants and everything in between.

MOUNTED POLICE OFFICER

You might wonder why our police force uses horses when we have fast cars and helicopters. But in certain situations, horses can be really useful to the police. I trained to be a police officer, and then after a few years, I moved to the mounted police unit. My horse, Apple, spent a year in training before joining the force. Together, we're a great team!

Armies also have mounted units, called the cavalry. It's been a long time since horses were used in battle, but they are still used in parades, ceremonies and displays.

1

My day starts at 7:00 a.m. at the stables. Our unit employs grooms to feed the horses and get the tack (the saddle, reins and stirrups) ready for the officers. But I like to saddle up myself as it gives me a chance to bond with Apple even more.

2

Our first job is to attend a protest march through the city center. I fasten a visor and nose guard to Apple. Sometimes, protesters throw things if they get angry, so I need to make sure Apple is protected.

3

Once we're at the march, Apple and I slowly walk beside the protesters. The crowd is very noisy, but Apple doesn't get nervous. He has been trained to stay calm in these situations.

4

I get a call on my radio about an argument between protesters close by. Apple is almost 6 feet tall, so when I sit on top of him, I can see everyone in the large crowd. I soon spot the troublemakers, and we reach them in no time. I make sure they go their separate ways, and the rest of the march goes smoothly.

5

After the march, Apple and I head off to our next job: to help manage the crowd at a soccer game. I've only ever been to one game where the fans became violent. But that soon stopped when they saw several large horses riding toward them! Luckily, the fans are very good-natured today—and they especially love Apple.

6

I arrive back at the stables after a long day. Most police officers can just change out of their uniform and head home, but I still have work to do. I remove Apple's tack and give him a good brush down before I leave him with the grooms. My job is hard work, but I wouldn't swap it for anything.

7

I usually head home at this point, but today is special—I'm going to an award ceremony. I'm being commended for saving a family involved in a car accident. I couldn't have done it without Apple, and I can't wait to show him the medal tomorrow—even if he's more interested in his breakfast!

MY JOB: BEST AND WORST PARTS

BEST: I love horses and get paid to spend all day with them.

WORST: I sometimes worry about the safety of my horse in a dangerous situation, such as an angry crowd.

ZOOKEEPER
(primates)

I look after the zoo's primates, which include gorillas, chimpanzees, orangutans, lemurs, capuchin monkeys, gibbons, baboons, macaques and marmosets. With over 50 animals, I am very busy! Luckily, I am part of a team of three primate keepers. I got a qualification in animal care before I applied for this job.

I have always wanted to work with primates, but there are many different kinds of zookeepers, including bird keepers, elephant keepers, big cat keepers, reptile keepers (see pages 38–39), marine animal keepers (who take care of penguins, seals and other sea animals) and hoof stock keepers (who specialize in hoofed animals such as giraffes and zebras).

1

The first job of the day is breakfast. Different primates have different needs, so I make sure each receives the right food. During this visit, I look for any signs of illness or injury. I know my animals better than anyone, and today I notice that one of the gibbons, Sally, is very quiet and sad looking. She is usually very energetic and playful, so I make a note of this for the zoo vet (see pages 32–33), who will check her later.

2

Next, the zoo vet joins me. Together, we give medicine to the animals that need it. Our orangutan, Chan, hates taking his medicine, so I hide it inside a banana, which he gobbles down happily.

3

I love my job, but not cleaning out the enclosures! However, the health of our primates is hugely important, so it must be done.

4

After lunch, a local school visits, and I give a talk. I love teaching people about primates. Every day, something different happens. Yesterday, a new chimpanzee arrived and needed help to settle in.

5

Primates are very intelligent and need lots to do, which makes my job different from other keepers'. Our zoo habitat designer often visits the enclosures to create interesting environments that mimic the ones in the natural world. The habitat designer makes sure there are plenty of things for the primates to climb and high places where they can sit, as they would in the wild.

6

Later in the afternoon, the larger primates have another feed. Bertie, our huge silverback gorilla, weighs as much as three adult humans and eats nearly 44 pounds of fruit, plants and vegetables every day.

7

The last hour is spent getting ready for tomorrow. This includes preparing the next day's food. With so many animals, there's a lot to prepare.

MY JOB: BEST AND WORST PARTS

BEST: I spend most of my day with the animals, building great friendships with them and learning all about their different characters. I love them all, especially the cheeky ones!

WORST: I do spend most of the day smelling like an ape!

8

Finally, I do one last check of the animals. Most days I finish at 5:00 p.m., but only if all the animals are happy, fed and back inside. I would never leave without my friends being ready for their evening's rest.